For Tim, who gave me the idea   D. B.

Ω

Published by
PEACHTREE PUBLISHERS, LTD.
1700 Chattahoochee Avenue
Atlanta, Georgia 30318-2112
www.peachtree-online.com

ISBN 1-56145-304-8

Text © 2004 by David Bedford
Illustrations © 2004 by Emily Bolam

First published by Oxford University Press in Great Britain, 2004

10 9 8 7 6 5 4 3 2 1
First Edition

Library of Congress Cataloging-in-Publication Data:

Bedford, David, 1969-
  The copy crocs / written by David Bedford ; illustrated by Emily Bolam.-- 1st ed.
      p. cm.
  Summary: Annoyed when the other crocodiles crowd and copy him, a young croc goes off
by himself, only to find that he sometimes enjoys the company around him.

ISBN 1-56145-304-8
[1. Crocodiles--Fiction. 2. Friendship--Fiction.] I. Bolam, Emily, ill. II. Title.
PZ7.B3817995 Co 2004
[E]--dc22   2003016531

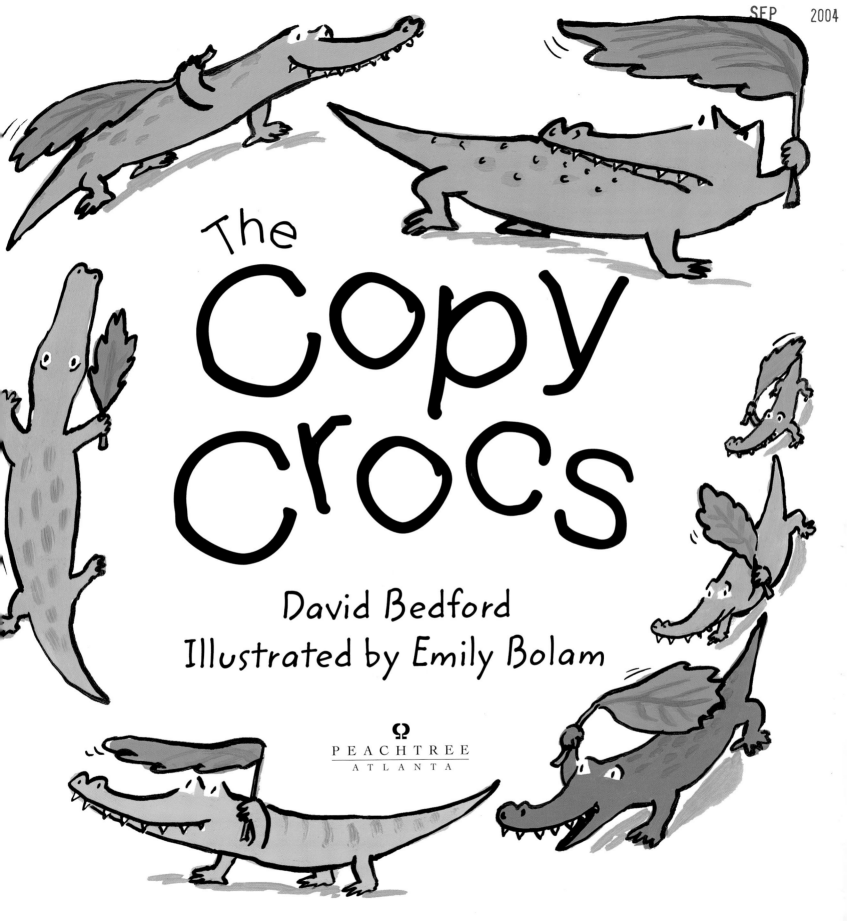

The Copy Crocs

David Bedford

Illustrated by Emily Bolam

PEACHTREE
ATLANTA

Crocodile had always lived
in the same pool and he liked it.
But he **didn't** like sharing it with all the other crocs.
Every time Crocodile moved, he bashed into someone.
And when the other crocs moved, they bashed him back.

"Stop pushing!" Crocodile shouted.
"You stop pushing!" said the other crocs.
It was too crowded, so Crocodile crawled out of his pool
and went to find somewhere else to live.

Crocodile found a new pool that was filled with slippery mud.

He liked it.

He really enjoyed sliding and rolling about.

But when the other crocs saw what Crocodile was doing…

…they started sliding and rolling about too.
"Stop copying me!" shouted Crocodile.
But the crocs said, "We can slide and roll if we want to.
It's not **your** pool."
Crocodile was so angry that he jumped out of his
muddy pool and ran away.

Crocodile found a place by the river
and stretched out in the sunshine.

He liked sunbathing.

But when he fell asleep…

...the other crocs came and sunbathed too!
It was so crowded that Crocodile could hardly move.
He was furious.
"Leave me alone!" he shouted.

Then he slipped into the cold river and swam away.

Crocodile found a floating log. He climbed on top of it,
kicked his feet, and glided down the river.
He liked watching the frogs and birds.

And he liked being on his own.

But then he heard a splashing sound and...

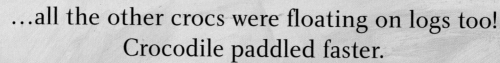

...all the other crocs were floating on logs too!
Crocodile paddled faster.
When he passed a bend in the river, he hid behind some bushes.
The copy crocs were having such a good time that they didn't see him.

Crocodile crept through the jungle until he
saw a mountain sitting all on its own.
"That's my kind of mountain!"
said Crocodile.

He started to climb.

At the top of the mountain,
there was only room for one crocodile.

Crocodile was happy.

But when the sun went down and it was getting dark...

...all the other crocs squeezed together
on Crocodile's mountain too!
"Why do you keep copying me?"
Crocodile shouted.
"Because you're always
doing new, fun things,"
said the other crocs.
"Anyway, we can sit
here if we want.
It's not **your**
mountain."

Crocodile
waited until
the other crocs
were sleeping. Then
he crept silently away…

...back to his pool.
Crocodile swam about
and didn't bash into anyone.
He never knew his pool was so **big.**

But Crocodile felt cold and lonely in the empty pool.
He remembered how it used to be packed with a
snug pile of snoring crocs.

"I wish my friends were here," said Crocodile sadly.

"SURPRISE!"

all the crocs shouted. "Here we are!"
They were laughing and bashing and rolling about.
Crocodile felt WONDERFUL.

He decided he **did** like sharing his pool
with the other crocs, even if
it was a bit of a squeeze.

But sometimes he liked to slip away...

...and do something **on his own,** before his friends found out...

...and joined in too!